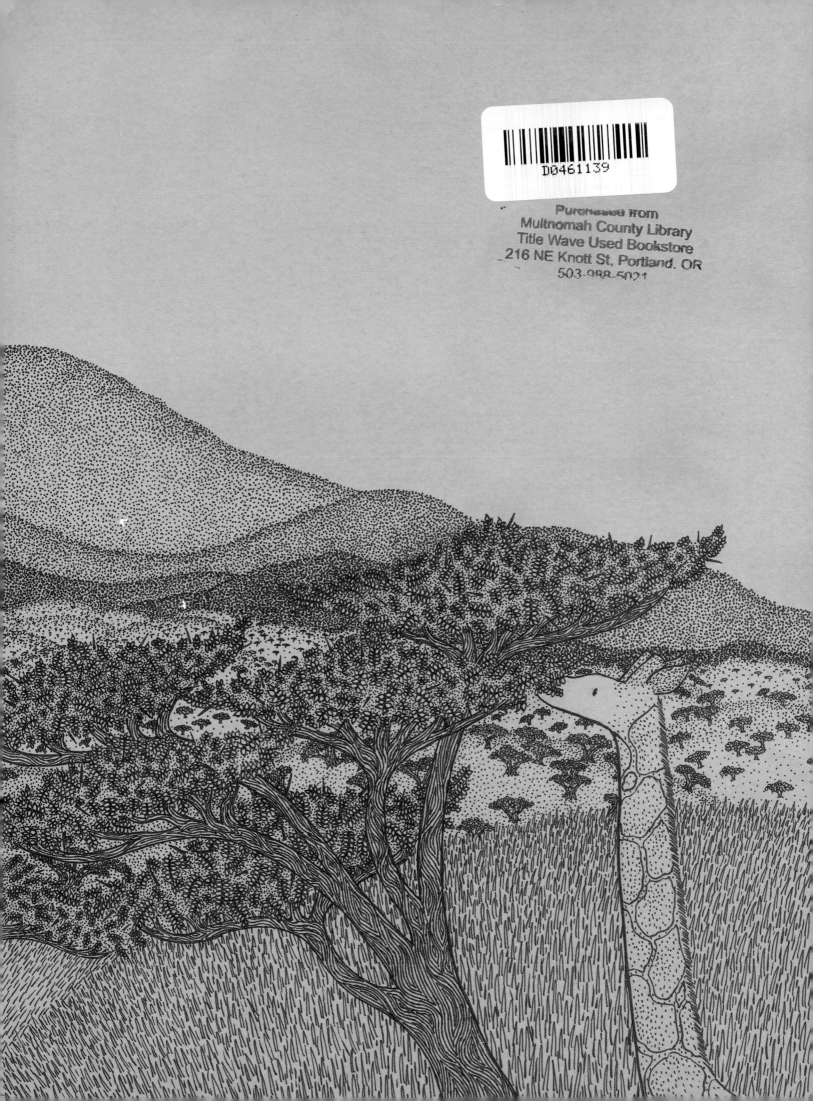

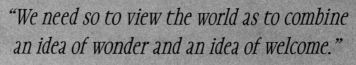

"We need so to view the world as to combine
an idea of wonder and an idea of welcome."
— G. K. Chesterton

In memory of Robert Hemminger

First edition 2015

Library of Congress Catalog Card Number 2014945455
ISBN 978-0-7636-7001-6

15 16 17 18 19 20 CCP 10 9 8 7 6 5 4 3 2 1

Printed in Shenzhen, Guangdong, China

This book was typeset in Integrity.
The illustrations were done in watercolor and ink.

Candlewick Press
99 Dover Street
Somerville, Massachusetts 02144

visit us at www.candlewick.com

The Song of Delphine

In the far reaches of the wild savannah
stood the palace of the great queen Theodora.

Kenneth Kraegel

Candlewick Press

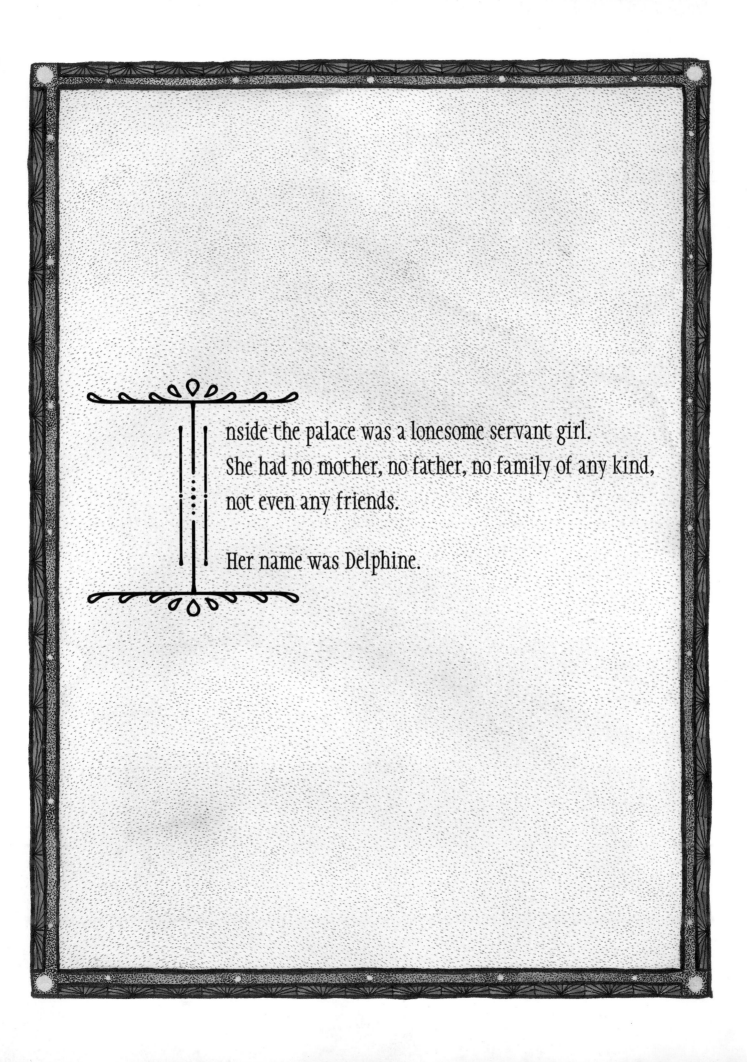

nside the palace was a lonesome servant girl.
She had no mother, no father, no family of any kind,
not even any friends.

Her name was Delphine.

From morning until night, she kept the palace clean and did whatever she was told to do.

It was not an easy life, but Delphine found it was easier if she sang. When her spirits were down, singing seemed to let some of the loneliness out.

One day, another girl came to live at the palace. It was the princess Beatrice, a niece of the queen. It was rumored that the princess had not gotten along with her new stepmother and so she had been sent to live with Queen Theodora.

Delphine was excited. How nice to have someone her age in the palace!

But having the princess around was not nice at all.

"Oh, Servant Girl, there goes your broom!
You should be careful where you leave it!"

"Servant Girl, you missed a spot!"

That night, frustrated and lonely, Delphine sang before she went to sleep. Soft and low, her song reached through the window, out into the dark savannah.

And in the dark savannah a pair of ears pricked up and heard every note that Delphine sang.

The next day was worse for Delphine.

"Servant Girl, look at this mess! Don't you know to clean off your feet before you come indoors?"

Then the princess kicked a ball into the next room.

"SERVANT GIRL! I cannot believe how clumsy you are! That mirror goes back generations! I will have to tell Queen Theodora about this!"

With heavy, worried tears, Delphine sang that night.

Certain that the queen would believe the princess, she sang and sang, letting the loneliness and fear pour out of her soul.

But when she opened her eyes, she was not alone at all!
A dozen curious, kind faces surrounded her, beckoning,
as if to say, "Come with us, come with us."

Gladly, Delphine went with them, out into the wild night air.
It was a wide new world for Delphine. She rode under the open sky
with these tall companions for hours and hours, savoring their
warm friendship and marveling at the wonders she saw.

When at last they came to a stop, Delphine sighed. "If I could, I would stay here forever. But I feel I must go back to the palace, come what may."

The giraffes curled around Delphine, hugging and nuzzling her affectionately.

When they arrived back at the palace, Delphine gave each giraffe a final hug.

"Good-bye, sweet friends. I hope you will come again very soon." And with that, they returned Delphine to her window.

But it was not her window!

"AAAHHH!" Princess Beatrice screamed. "HELP! HELP! What are you doing in my room? How did you get in my window?"

Delphine was stunned. "Oh, dear! I didn't mean . . . Princess, I am very sorry. I —"

"You *will* be very sorry!" the princess roared. "The queen will know about this for sure! *HELP!*"

Delphine's heart pounded. All seemed lost.

In the midst of the confusion, Delphine happened to notice a portrait by the princess's bed. It was a painting of the princess's late mother.

"I never knew my mother," Delphine said softly. "You must miss yours terribly." The princess stared hard at Delphine.

"When I am feeling lonesome, there is a song that I like to sing," said Delphine. "It goes like this. . . ." And, almost whispering at first, Delphine sang. Steadily, her voice grew stronger and stronger, filling the room with sound and feeling.

But before Delphine could finish, guards burst into the room and carried her away.

Locked up and all alone, Delphine tried to sing, but no song came.

Later that morning, Delphine was brought before the queen.

"Princess Beatrice tells me that you sing," the queen said.

Delphine nodded.

"Would you sing for us now?"

Delphine looked up. What could this mean?
With a trembling heart, Delphine sang. When she finished,
Queen Theodora sighed contentedly.

"Ah, Delphine, that was lovely, just lovely. It set my heart at ease.
From now on, I would like you to be my singer. There will be no
more scrubbing floors for you, my dear."

With that, the queen took her leave.

Once again, Delphine and the princess were alone.

"Princess, I am sorry I —" Delphine began. But the princess cut her off.

"I am the one who should apologize. What you said was true: I am lonely — lonely and sad. But the song you sang was beautiful. It said what I have been wanting to say. Thank you for being so kind, even when I have been so cruel."

Delphine stared at the princess in astonishment.

"Now," said the princess, breaking into a broad smile, "would you *please* tell me how you managed to get in my window? I haven't been able to figure it out!"

Delphine laughed. "I will do better than that, Princess," she said. "Tonight I will *show* you!"

So, late that night (and on many, many nights to come), Delphine sang out the window, calling her dear friends the giraffes. Then out they went, the princess, Delphine, and the giraffes, rambling into the far reaches of the wild savannah, all of them, together.